# A Guide to the Edibles
## of the Seashore

by Catherine Derevitzky

# Introduction

This is a guide to common edible plants and creatures found along the New England seashore.

Included are seaside plants, both edible and medicinal, seaweed, shellfish, crustaceans, and a few species of fish that can be caught off piers or shore. Each plant and animal is illustrated for identification. Its common location is given along with a simple method of preparation.

# Contents

## Bayberry

Bayberry is a common shrub that grows in sandy soil above the tide line.

In the fall, clusters of hard, aromatic berries may be easily gathered to make candles or soap.

To obtain the wax, boil the berries in a large pot for about ten minutes, then strain to remove all the used berries. As the water cools, the greenish blue wax will harden on the surface. This wax can then be remelted for candles or soap.

To make candles, melt the wax in a tall can. Next tie candle wicks to a stick and lower them into the wax. Lift out and wait for the wax to harden. Repeat this process until you have a candle of the size you want.

Before the last dip, to have smoother candles, shave off with a knife the uneven edges. About one pound of

wax is needed to make six candles. Bayberry candles are more brittle and less greasy than those made from tallow.

To make six bars of soap, dissolve two tbsp. of lye in one third cup cold water. Use enamel or iron utensils and spoon. Do not use aluminum.

The lye will heat up the water. Wait for the container to cool to lukewarm. Never test the liquid with your fingers. Next pour the lye solution in to one cup of melted wax. Stir slowly for 15-20 minutes. Pour into molds and keep in a warm place for three days. For molds you can use a flat enamel pan. The soap will be mild with a pleasant fragrance of Bayberry.

Bayberry leaf tea makes a pleasant drink. It is also astringent which makes it a good gargle for a sore throat or remedy for diarrhea.

Steep a teaspoonful in a pint of boiling water for 15-20 minutes and drink warm. The aromatic leaves may also be used in cooking. They add a good flavor to soups and stews.

growing in sand above the high tide line.

The blossoms are followed by peapods which should be picked while they are still bright green, or the little peas will be tasteless.

Cook them in boiling water for about ten to twelve minutes till tender. Then drain and serve with butter and salt.

### Beach Pea

This plant grows to a foot in height and looks much like the garden pea.

It blooms from June to August, and is found

## Scurvy Grass

Also a member of the mustard family, found growing along rocky beaches. A small plant with fleshy leaves which can be obtained all year round as long as there is no snow.

It is a pleasant tasting wild green that can be added raw to salads or boiled for a few minutes, then served with butter. Very high in vitamin C.

Early sailors found that a tea made of the plant prevented scurvy.

## Sea Rocket

A member of the mustard family, growing to a height of two ft. Found on sandy and rocky shores. The whole plant, with its fleshy leaves, is tasty if cooked like spinach or added raw to meat sandwiches. Tastes like mustard and horse radish.

Very rich in vitamins and minerals.

7.

## Clotburr

Growing to a height of one to two feet, Clotburr is found on the upper beach.

It derives its name from its ability to clot blood. Any part of the plant may be used. Mash or chew into a pulp and apply to cuts to stop bleeding. Apply a whole leaf to cover pulp and bind with a bandage.

## Silverweed

Found in marshes growing on clay ground above the high tide line. The whole plant is astringent with the roots being the strongest.

Make a tea using 1 oz. of the plant to two cups boiling water. Let steep about 10 min. Sweeten with honey. This is a good gargle for sore throats and is helpful when used for ulcers and sores of the mouth.

The roots, dug in the spring, resemble parsnips in taste. Wash and boil them for a few minutes, then serve with butter.

## Goosetongue

This relative of the common plantain grows on clay shores and in cracks and crevices in rocks along the seashore.

The slender, fleshy leaves resemble thick, brittle grass blades and grow to a height of six to eight inches.

They make a good, nutritious cooked vegetable. Break the leaves in pieces and boil for about fifteen minutes. Drain and serve with butter.

## Sea Spinach

Also known as Orache, is a relative of the garden spinach. It is very abundant just above the high tide line.

The mealy leaves are good in salads or excellent as a slightly salty cooked green. Just boil the leaves in a little water for about 5 min. and serve with butter. The greens cook down alot.

The young leaves may be gathered as the plant puts out new growth, spring through fall. It is very rich in vitamins and sea salt minerals.

## Sow Thistle

Found growing on rocky beaches. The young leaves are very rich in minerals. They may be cooked and eaten as spinach or added raw to salads.

The white milk expressed from the stems may be applied to sunburns to relieve the pain.

## Sea Blite

There are five species that look very much alike and all are edible. The whole plant is succulent and tender. It is edible spring through the end of summer.

Chop the greens and boil five minutes; then drain and serve with butter.

Very pleasant flavor, slightly salty.

May be added to soups and stews or chopped to salads.

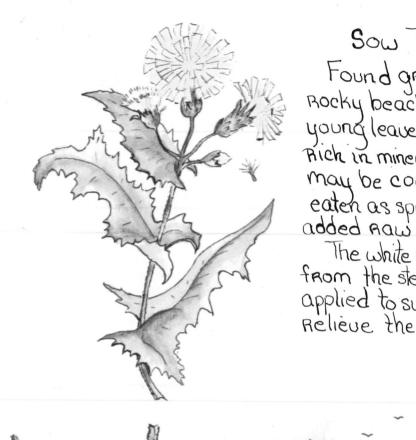

BUTTER

# Glassworth

Also known as Samphire weed, is a relative of spinach. There are three species of this plant, all look much alike and all are edible. They grow in patches on clay shores and in salt marshes, just above the high tide line.

The plant is good to eat spring through fall when the top growth can be picked. The juicy, translucent stems are tasty raw, added to salads, or boiled five minutes and eaten with butter.

In the lower stems there is a hard, twig center which can be easily pulled out after it is cooked.

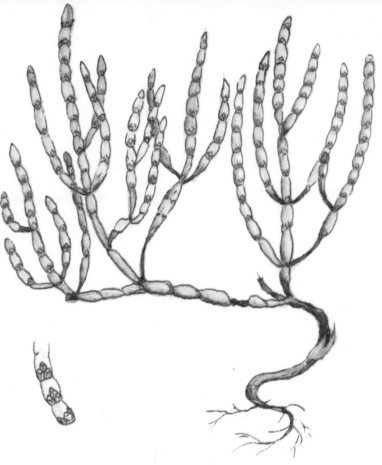

## Glassworth Pickles

Cook the plant and pull out the hard stringy center.

Make a marinade of two cups vinegar to two cups sugar. Bring it to a boil to dissolve the sugar. Pour the marinade over the Glassworth which has been packed in jars. Seal.

Delicious with boiled potatoes.

11

## Sea Lavender

Found growing in saltmarshes and on clayshores. Flowers from August to October.

The root and flowers are a strong astringent used to check dysentery and diarrhea, and in the treatment of wounds and cuts. Steep a handful of the flowers in a quart of boiling water and take a few sips morning and night. For wounds, apply crushed flowers directly to the cut.

## Jelly

Crush 6 lbs. of ripe plums. Put them in a kettle, add two cups of water, and simmer for about ten minutes. Strain through a cheesecloth. Add a box of pectin to the juice, bring to a boil, and add 8 cups of sugar.

Stir until sugar dissolves. Bring to a boil and boil for ten minutes. Then pour into jelly glasses and cover with paraffin.

## Beach Plum

A low shrub that grows in dune sand. The fruit are very abundant and usually the size and color of Concord Grapes. The plums ripen in September. They may be very sweet, or very seedy and dry, but always make a good tart jelly or preserves.

## Salt Spray Rose

This shrub grows to a height of six feet along sandy and rocky shores. The sweet flavored rose hip ripens in August and September. It is extremely rich in vitamin C.

### Rose Hip Jam

Cut rosehips in half and remove seedy center. Grind five cups of cleaned rose hips. Add three cups of water. Boil for twenty minutes in a covered pan. Then rub through a sieve. Add the juice of one lemon to the puree. Stir in three and a half cups sugar. Cook until thick. Fill hot, sterilized jars and seal.

Half a cup of rose hips has twenty five times the vitamin c content of the same amount of orange juice.

# Rockweed

There are many species of this alga but they all look much alike. It grows on rocks exposed at low tide. Fronds are two-three feet long.

Rockweed is a very valuable green manure and fertilizer for potatoes and other crops. Good source of potash. Gather from the rocks and spread on land to plough in. It should not be left laying in heaps as rotting liberates the potash which may be wasted. Fresh seaweed contains 20-40 lbs. of potash to the ton.

# Irish Moss

Irish Moss is very rich in sulphur and Iodine. For a nourishing aspic salad, take about a cupful of fresh moss and wash it in several waters to remove a fishy taste. Cover with water and boil for a few minutes. Allow to cool and then stir in chopped Sea Blite, Glassworth, and Sea Rocket. Pour into a mold or bowl and allow to set in a cool place.

Carrageen is the gelatinous extract of this plant used in confectionery and bakery firms.

Found at, or just below the low tide level, carpeting rocky tide pools. When cast up on shore it becomes bleached by the sun. When fresh it is tough, and drying makes it tougher. It becomes tender only after being boiled for a few minutes. Chop the plants and add to soups and stews. This will add body as okra would.

## Edible Kelp

Found growing on rocky ledges at low tide. It is distinguished from other kelps by short, ribless fronds growing at the base of the main stem and a midrib in the main frond. The main frond is one to ten feet long.

Dry the fronds thoroughly in an oven on very low heat, with the door ajar. Pack loosely in jars after shredding with a sharp knife.

To use as a seasoning, pound into a powder and place in a salt shaker. Good in soups and stews, on potatoes and other vegetables. Kelp is rich in iodine and many other trace minerals needed for health.

## Dulse

Found near the low tide line and deeper, attached to rocks and shells.

It is tough when raw, but if dried for about a week, it becomes tender with a salty sea flavor. When dried, Dulse becomes dark, greenish black with a dusting of sea salt.

Good to nibble on, and the flavor is brought out by long chewing. It is a rich source of Iodine. May be shredded finely and added to chowders.

17.

18

# Razor Clams

Found in sand at lowtide. The average length is 6-7 inches. The colonies may be found by little rectangular holes at the waters edge.

The clams may be brought up by a spade, but you must work quickly as they burrow very rapidly. To escape predators they burrow under ground by pushing the sand aside with their foot. Another way to catch them is to put salt in their burrows and then grab them with your fingers when they come up.

They are delicious steamed. Wash the shells, put in a kettle with a little water and steam for about 10 minutes or until they open. Then dip in butter and eat. The cooked meat may also be chopped and used in clam chowders.

## Periwinkles

Found in large numbers on rocky coasts, crawling over seaweed at lowtide. Usually about one inch in diameter.

Boil them for a few minutes in water with a little salt added to it. The salt toughens the meat so it can be removed in one piece.

When the operculum (hard little door) drops off and the creature protrudes it is cooked.

Remove with a toothpick, dip in butter and eat.

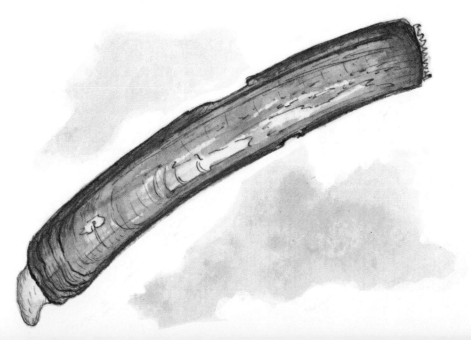

# Mussels

The Blue Mussel is very abundant and easy to gather in many places at low tide.

It is found on rocky shores, pilings, and in clumps in mud flats. Adult mussels are about three inches long. They attach themselves with very strong threads called byssus or beard. Do not take unattached mussels as they are probably dead. Before steaming the mussel, pull out the beard by pulling it hard toward the large end of the shell. Gather about two dozen mussels for each person. Place mussels in a kettle with a little water, about two cups. Bring to a boil and steam till all the shells are open. Dip in melted butter and enjoy.

Mussels are rich in vitamins and minerals and are a very good source of protein that is low in fat.

Never pick mussels or any other shellfish in or near very settled areas as the water is probably very polluted. Shellfish readily accumulate pollutants while filtering water for oxygen and nutrients.

# Mussel Spaghetti

2  8 oz. cans tomato sauce

1  large onion, chopped

2  cloves garlic, minced

handful of dry, crushed celery leaves

3 tbsp. vinegar

1 tbsp. sugar

1/4 cup soy sauce

1/3 cup olive oil

1 tsp. oregano

1 tsp. basil

6 dozen steamed mussels (save broth)

Combine all ingredients except mussels and simmer for a half an hour. Remove mussels from shells, chop in half and add to sauce. Simmer for another half hour.

Use the water which the mussels had been steamed in to cook the spaghetti. Pour it into a kettle, being carefull towards the end as it will have a little sand on the bottom. The broth will be bluish in color. Add needed amount of water, bring to a boil, and cook spaghetti. The mussel broth imparts a good flavor to the pasta. Drain and serve with sauce. Serves 3 or 4.

# Soft Shell Clams
### or Steamers

Found in tidal mud flats at low tide, usually at a depth of five to eight inches. When walking across the flat they often squirt under your footsteps as they withdraw their siphon. Dig beneath patches of holes left by the siphons. A garden spading fork or even a flat rock may be used.

The clam may grow to a length of five inches but is usually found in the two to three inch size.

The shell is very brittle and breaks easily, which is a problem in digging. To steam, wash shells to free of mud. Place in a kettle with two cups of water, cover, and bring to a boil. Steam till the shells open. Serve with a dish of melted butter and a cup of clam broth; the liquor from the kettle. Allow two dozen clams per person.

# Clam Chowder

4-5 dozen clams, steamed
(save broth)
1 cup cream / 1 cup milk, scalded
3 large onions, sliced in rings
1 quart boiling water
2 stalks celery, minced
2 carrots diced
2 tbsp. parsley, chopped
½ tsp. thyme
2 large bayberry leaves
1 tsp. salt
3 large potatoes, peeled + cubed

Roux:
2 rounded tbsp. flour
2 rounded tbsp. butter
Dash of Tobasco Sauce

Brown onions. Put onions, clam broth, and one quart boiling water in a kettle. Add celery, carrots, parsley, thyme, bayberry, salt, and let mixture come to a boil

Reduce to simmering and add the potatoes. Prepare roux by browning the flour in the butter. Make it creamy and smooth by stirring in broth from the kettle. Stir in the milk and cream.

Chop clams in half and add to the kettle before the potatoes start to soften.

Simmer slowly till the potatoes are just tender, then stir in the roux and add a dash of Tobasco Sauce.

23.

## Hen Clams

the sand. Hands or toes may be used to bring them up. The shell grows to a length of 7 in. but anything less than 4 in. is not worth bothering with as only the muscles are good to eat. These are an inch in diameter, tender and tasty.

Clean the clams on the beach so the gulls can have the rest of the clam and there is no waste. Where the siphon protrudes there is a small opening between the two shells. Insert a knife and slide it under the muscle where it fastens to the shell. Open over a bowl to catch the juice, then cut the muscle on the opposite shell. Wash the two little pieces of meat in the clam juice, roll in bread crumbs and fry in some butter. The meat and juice are also good for making clam chowder.

This clam, also known as Surf Clam, is found in large numbers at the level of the lowest tides on most sandy, surf washed beaches.

They are easiest to gather after the full or new moon when the tides are the greatest, called spring tides.

These clams do not bury deeply and so are found just under the surface of

## Eastern Oyster

Found in bays and tidal creeks, below the low-water line, attached to other shells and rocks. Shells are rough and 3 to 5 inches in size.

The oyster is in season only during the month with an "R" in them.

To open, break off excess shell so you can slip a knife in, slide it back and cut the hinge muscle. Then pull the flat side of the shell off.

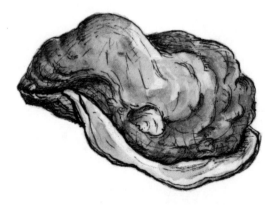

Pearls produced by edible oysters are of little value.

Now you can cut the oyster from the rounded side of the shell.

Oysters may be served raw on the half shell or be fried or stewed.

## Oyster Stew

Cook two cups oysters in 3 tbsp. butter till the edges curl. Add 3 cups milk and 1 cup cream, liquid from the oysters, a bayberry leaf and 1 tsp. salt. Heat till bubbles form around the edge of the pan. Do not boil.    Serve with crackers.

# Quahogs

Also known as Hard Shell Clams, they measure four to five inches across when full grown. When young, one and a half to three inches, they are called Cherrystones.

These clams are usually found in mud and sand shores of inlets in low water at lowtide. Because they have short siphons they lay just below the surface. While wading waistdeep in water, you can feel around with your toes for clams underfoot and then easily bring them up that way. They are usually found in groups.

While they are small, as Cherrystones, they are best steamed. Put the clams in a kettle with a little water. Bring to a boil and steam for about twenty minutes untill all the clams open. Remove from the shell, dip in butter and eat. The meat is both sweeter and saltier than that of soft shell clams.

Large clams are tough, so are best stuffed or in chowders. Use the same recipe as for steamers, using about two dozen steamed clams. Put the clams through a meat grinder before adding to the chowder.

2

Stuffed Quahogs.     Steam two dozen clams and then grind in a meat grinder. Add half a cup of minced onion, a chopped green pepper, a clove of minced garlic and two cups bread crumbs. Dampen the stuffing with the clam broth from the kettle and mix. Fill twelve half shells with the mixture and bake at 450°.     OR, you can cover with the other half shell, wrap in aluminum foil, and bake in hot coals in a campfire.

The purple splotches on the inside of the shell was the material that the Indians made their most valuable wampum from.

# Scallops

The Bay Scallop is from 2½" inches to 3 inches across and ordinarily prefers sheltered shores. The Deep Sea Scallop grows to 8 inches across and is found in waters up to 300 feet deep. All the species Resemble each other and are easily Recognized. A good scallop bed is usually betrayed by an abundance of dead scallop shells on the shore. Patches of eel grass at

Deep Sea Scallop

Bay Scallop

low tide are a good place to hunt for them. On a calm day when the water is still, drift slowly over the area in a Row boat and search the bottom. When found at a depth of 10 to 12 feet they may be scooped up with a long handled dip net.

When captured, the scallop will beat its values wildly in an attempt to escape. Commercially only the musele is sold, however the whole crea-ture is good to eat when freshly caught.

To open, slide a sharp knife between the values and cut the muscle where it joins one value. Remove it and eat it separately or cook the whole creature

2

If using the entire scallop, chop coarsely to make three cups of meat. Add three fourths of a cup of cream, one half cup chopped onion, one cup bread crumbs and salt to taste. Mix and fill scallop shells with this mixture. Bake at 350° for a half an hour.

If using scallop muscles only, place 4 cups of scallops in a bowl, pour one quart boiling water over them and add 2 tbsp. vinegar. Let stand for 5 min. and drain. Roll scallops in bread crumbs, dip in beaten egg (2 eggs) and again in bread crumbs. Place in a single layer in a shallow baking pan, with a layer of onions and garlic that have been browned in butter on the bottom. Bake in a hot oven till crumbs brown. About 10-12 minutes.

The scallop swims through water at good speed by rapidly opening and closing its valves and squirting water through openings in its mantle cavity.

it is quite tasty if properly prepared. Crack the shell with a hammer and remove the creature. Cut off the operculum (door) and slice the foot in 1/2 inch thick pieces. Discard the remains. Pound the meat with a wooden mallet and sprinkle with meat tenderizer, then set in the refrigerator for a day. The meat will be rubbery if this is not done. When ready to eat, dip each piece in a beaten egg, roll in bread crumbs and fry in some butter.

## Moon Shell

Usually two to three inches in diameter, they may be found in shallow water at lowtide. Sometimes all you will see is a round mound of sand in which they hide. Their tremendous foot does not look like it would ever fit inside its shell, but

# Crustaceans

## Lobster

The lobster, a seafood favorite, is found on rocky and sandy bottoms from shallow to very deep water.

They are caught in wooden traps, or pots, baited with dead fish. The size and taking of lobsters is strictly regulated by law in every state. The average weight of the lobsters caught is one to two lbs. although they grow much larger.

Boiled lobster. Bring water to a boil in a large kettle. Plunge live lobsters in head first. Bring water back to a boil, reduce heat, and simmer for 15 minutes if lobster is one pound size. If one and a half, simmer another 5 minutes. Remove from kettle, place lobster on its back and split the body lengthwise. Remove the dark vein and small sac just below the head. Leave the green liver and any red roe. Next crack the large claws. Eat with melted butter. Cold lobster is good with mayonnaise.

## Rock Crab

A common crab found along rocky shores in shallow water just below the low tide line or hiding among rocks in seaweed. The average size is three to four inches across at the carapace. Another species that is very similar in appearance is the Jonah crab. It is a little larger, heavier and has a rougher shell.

Both crabs may be caught with baited lines from floating docks using a piece of fish or clam for bait. Also look for crabs at low tide around grassy tide pools where they may be scooped up with a dip net. Nighttime is especially good for this as they are more bold at this time.

The simplest way to prepare crabs is to have them boiled. Drop crabs in boiling water and cook for about 15 to 20 minutes. Drain and fill kettle with cold water to cool the crabs. To eat, remove the claws and legs. Crack them with a pair of pliers or a nutcracker. Then pick out the

the meat. Next turn the crab over and lift the "tail" from its recess and tear it away. Pull upper and lower shells apart and throw away the top shell. Remove gills and all the spongy material. Then break the body in half, wash the two pieces and pick out the meat. Dip in mayonnaise and eat.

Mayonnaise: In a small bowl beat two egg yolks and one tsp. salt till thick and lemon colored. Add one cup oil in a thin stream beating till thick. Slowly add two tbsp. vinegar, two tsp. sugar and 1 clove garlic, minced, beating constantly. Refrigerate until ready to use. Garlic makes this "Sauce Provencale".

To remove the egg sacs, or Roe, crack the shell in half with several blows of a hammer. The Roe is usually bright orange in color and found in the center of the upper shell. Remove it with a spoon as it will leave a stain on your fingers which is hard to wash off.

The Roe may be cooked, but is best eaten raw on crackers. It is nourishing and a good source of protein.

## Sea Urchins

Sea Urchins are a relative of the starfish found in tidepools at the low water line. The body is 2 to 2½ inches in diameter with movable ½ inch spines all over it.

The best time to gather them is from July to December when more of the urchins will have egg sacs, which is the edible part.

The several species of fish mentioned here are only a few of the many that swim close to shore and can be easily caught from wharves, rocky points and old bridges with very simple inexpensive equipment.

## Winter Flounder

This is the most common shallow water flounder. It likes sandy or mud bottoms and goes up rivers almost to fresh water. The body is flattened so that the fish rests on one side on the bottom. The underside is white. It may be caught from boat or shore with a variety of baits. Pieces of sea worms, clams may be used with a long shank no. 8 or no. 10 hook. Little pieces of smoked fish also work very well. Average size is one pound.

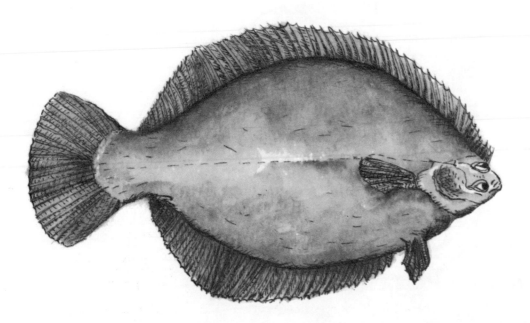

Flounder may be filleted but is even more flavorful if fried whole. Remove entrails and cut tail, fins, and head off leaving you with a square shaped piece.

Dip in beaten egg and then roll in bread crumbs. Fry in a greased frying pan.

## Mackerel

This is an open ocean fish that moves in large schools. Every spring, near Cape Hatteras, they start out on a northward journey and continue to move up along the coast as summer progresses.

When a mackerel school is in the area, they can be caught in large numbers in a short amount of

time with just a handline and shiny diamond jig. A no. 8 hook with a piece of mackerel for bait also works well. The average weight of fish caught is one pound.

Mackerel may be baked, broiled or fried. As it is a very fatty fish it is best broiled. Remove entrails, cut head off and wash the fish.

Arrange on a rack four inches from the heat, put a tablespoonful of chopped onion in the cavity, and broil until fish flakes easily when tested with a fork. Baste with lemon juice.

Serve this tasty fish with rice and soy sauce.

## Smelt

A small, sweet fleshed fish that enter rivers and streams in large schools during the winter months to spawn.

The average length is eight inches. Smelt are easily caught by hook and line from wharves, bridges and through ice. Use a no. 8 hook with clams or worms for bait.

To prepare the fish, cut the head off and remove the entrails.

Grease a frying pan and fry. Smelt need no coating.

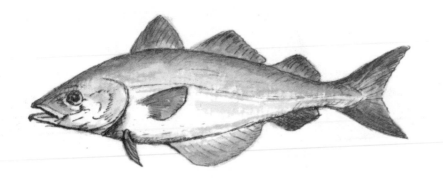

## Pollack

A very common fish, averaging one to three pounds in weight, that is a member of the Cod family. Pollack will bite on anything. A jig or a no. 8 hook may be used.

As the fish is full of small bones it should be filleted.

With a sharp pointed knife make a slit down each side of the fish just behind the gills. Make two slits through the skin down the back from the head to the tail. One on each side of the dorsal fin. Peel the skin back. Remove the flesh from the backbone by sliding the knife just outside the bones along the back. Then cut along the median line and remove the fillet. Repeat process on other side. The fillets are good fried, broiled, or baked.

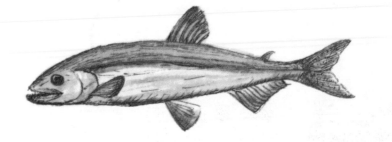

# Common Skate

This member of the shark family is commonly caught when fishing for flounder from a wharf. It likes smooth, shallow bottoms where it is easy to stir up a cloud of sand or mud with a flap of the wings and then settle in it. From this position they feed by snapping up a passing crab or mollusk. Skate rarely reach the length of two feet.

When you land one, kill it by a hard blow between the eyes and then cut off the wings close to the body. To clean a wing for cooking, cut it in one inch wide strips. Then remove the skin from these strips and slice the meat from each side of the cartilage.

These delicious slender fillets can be cooked as any fish fillet or may be cut in one inch squares and then cooked like scallops.

In flesh and flavor the meat very much resembles scallop muscles.

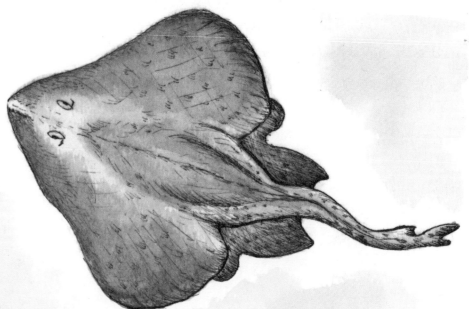

# Clambake

In a clambake food is cooked by steam coming from wet seaweed that has been placed on hot rocks heated by a fire. The contents of a clambake depends on the foods available and the preferences of those participating. Lobsters, clams, corn in the husk and potatoes are the usual ingredients, however, crabs, mussels, and other shellfish may be added.

Dig a circular hole two feet deep by three feet long above the high tide line. Line it with smooth rocks. Next, pile driftwood on top for a bonfire. Light it and let it burn down to coals. Place a layer of Rockweed over the coals about five inches deep, place all the food on the seaweed and another layer of seaweed over all. Cover this with a piece of canvas to keep the steam in. Weigh down the edges with rocks. Let bake for about an hour. Remove canvas and top layer of seaweed and you are ready to pile high your picnic plates. Have dishes of melted butter handy.

# INDEX